# SHINING LEGACY

**Storypoems for the Young,
So Black Heroes and Heroines Forever Will Be Sung**

by Nkechi Taifa

Illustrator Mary E. Mudiku (Maesgara)

Original Black and White Illustrations Colorized by Free BenJamin

2021 COLOR EDITION

Published by the House of Songhay II
Washington, DC
www.NkechiTaifa.com

## DEDICATION

Dedicated to NationHouse Watoto School for it was through the influence of that Independent Black Institution where many of my storypoems were inspired and created when I taught there between 1977-1980.


## ACKNOWLEDGEMENTS

I am grateful to Free BenJamin for her expertise in colorizing the original black and white illustrations, and for graphic design and layout.

# TABLE OF CONTENTS


Introduction ............................................................................................... 1

**STORYPOEMS**

The Prophecy of the Coming of the Paleface – An Epic Tale ............................ 7

Cinque and the Amistad ................................................................................. 15

The Saga of Toussaint L'Ouverture ................................................................. 17

The Legend of Denmark Vesey ....................................................................... 21

Harriet Was Strong, She Never Went Wrong ................................................... 29

Sojourner's Truth ........................................................................................... 33

The Mighty Marcus Garvey ............................................................................ 35

Celebrating Paul Robeson .............................................................................. 37

Her Name Was Fannie Lou Hamer .................................................................. 39

The Ballad of Rosa Parks ................................................................................ 43

John Coltrane Played All That Jazz .................................................................. 47

The Saga of Malcolm X ................................................................................... 49

African Proverbs ............................................................................................. 58

**GLOSSARY** .............................................................................................. 59

**REVIEW QUESTIONS AND WORK PROJECTS** ............................................ 62

# INTRODUCTION

This color edition of *Shining Legacy* comes 38 years after the original 1983 black and white publication. In 1983, the Martin Luther King, Jr. holiday became a federal law, honoring the slain civil rights leader. Today, nearly 40 years later, Juneteenth, which recognizes when the last enslaved persons learned of their freedom, has become a federal holiday. Yet although Black elected officials, entrepreneurs and entertainers have achieved enormous success, little has changed for the Black masses.

*Shining Legacy* is timeless. I wrote this book as a young teacher in an Independent Black School during the late '70s, before I entered law school. During those days there were not many books about historic Black leaders for youth, and I wanted my first-grade students to not only have stories, images and ideas that belonged to them, but also those that represented freedom fighters.

The book's 1983 introduction quoted my mentor in the Black liberation movement, Imari Abubakari Obadele, who stressed that we did not need "to highlight the 'Tontos' of our race – those who assisted in their own enslavement and destruction." What we needed to do was to "highlight the freedom fighters, those who struggled unceasingly and demanded freedom." I took Brother Imari's quote to heart, and within *Shining Legacy* highlighted a few of these uncompromising heroes and heroines, some whose names during that time did not automatically surface. Inspired by historian J.A. Rogers, I did so in a motivating way, so that retaining historical data was not a brainwashing drudgery, but an inspiring joy, as I weaved biographical information into moving stories accentuated with rhyme. Thus, the appellation, "storypoems."

*Shining Legacy* showcases freedom fighters that were under-represented in books for young people at the time, such as Denmark Vesey, who master-minded an elaborate rebellion to free enslaved people, and Joseph Cinque, who led a rebellion on the slave ship, Amistad. I highlight Paul Robeson and Marcus Garvey, and embrace the military genius Toussaint L'Ouverture. My book also features enlightening storypoems high-lighting freedom-fighting women – Harriet Tubman, Sojourner Truth, Fannie Lou Hamer, and Rosa Parks. Finally, I include the story of the hero pivotal to my consciousness, Malcolm X.

Through *Shining Legacy* I seek to provide much-needed identity, purpose and direction for Black youth through original epics, ballads, sagas and tales depicting Black historical and cultural wealth; and poignant illustrations bring these freedom fighters of the past to life.

The original publication of *Shining Legacy* was so popular it went through multiple printings, and was a mainstay in Black bookstores nationwide and even internationally from the early '80s through the '90s, during a time when Black children's books were conspicuously scarce. Thankfully, today, a look down the aisle of bookstores, both Black and mainstream establishments, reveal a wide array of literature for children and young people written by and about Black people, and I'm proud to have been one of the early pioneers who sought to make a difference. Indeed, the support my early books received over the years from scores of Black bookstores and distributors was the foundation behind today's top sales rankings of my memoir, *Black Power/Black Lawyer: My Audacious Quest for Justice*.

I'm re-publishing my books from the past at this time because I think current systematic attacks across the country against teaching the true history of Black people in America in the midst of a pandemic of white supremacy will damage the future of our children. Black youth need uplifting, unplugged material that allows them to see themselves in their most positive light, not as a social problem or controversy, and motivates them to learn more.

Many of the young people who read my books during the 80s and 90s now have children of their own. So there are new generations and new audiences today as I dust off my books and seek to resurrect my take on Black history, ancient and modern.

Some of the concepts within *Shining Legacy* were inspired and influenced by various people and events. The concept of "The Way" expressed in the epic "The Prophecy of the Coming of the Paleface" was inspired by Ayi Kwei Armah's brilliant *Two Thousand Seasons*. Much of the research from "The Legend of Denmark Vesey" emanated from John Oliver Killens' *Great Gitting Up Morning* and *The Trial Record of Denmark Vesey*. "The Mighty Marcus Garvey" was inspired by my Uncle Ambrose from New York, who passed on to me the stories his father passed to him about Garvey's parades and the shares he had purchased in the Black Star Line.

"John Coltrane played all that Jazz" was motivated by a discussion one Kwanzaa evening between Brother Rasafik Wesui, Maulana Douglas Jones, and Reverend Ishakamusa Barashango, who iterated to me the importance of integrating Black music with Black history. "Cinque and the Amistad" is dedicated to the 150+ million African captives who lost their lives in the MAAFA of the Middle Passage and slavery. "The Ballad of Rosa Parks," "Harriet Was Strong, She Never Went Wrong," "Her Name was Fannie Lou Hamer," and "Sojourner's Truth," are all a testament to the tradition and richness that constitutes Black womanhood.

Since the first edition, we have lost many, many warriors in the struggle for social justice, including the names of many of the people just listed above. As they were inspired by those who came before them, I pray that today's youth are inspired by the entire gamut of noble Black men and women, those within these pages and those in the streets right now, awaiting their own entries. Once *Shining Legacy*'s readers connect with the collective genealogy that fuses past with present, I am confident they will forge future paths for freedom that, in this historical moment, surpasses current visions.

**Nkechi Taifa**

**Washington, D.C., June 2021**

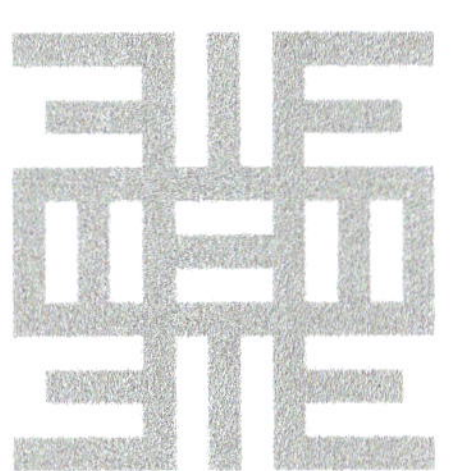

# STORYPOEMS

# THE PROPHECY OF THE COMING OF THE PALEFACE

***An Epic Tale***


"Mama, mama can I go out today
Down by the river, to catch some fish and play?"

"Well my ebony child. Just for a while.
Return at the drum's beat. Our village is going to meet."

"You are very kind my mother. I will do as you wish.
When I hear the drums talk, I'll come home with my fish."

Skipping through the bush, happy as can be.
He sees an elder coming with a limp in his knee.

"Who do you be," the elder asks, "so happy and carefree?
I see you're alone, yet unafraid. You must learn many things
with your age-grade."

"No, I'm not afraid. And neither is my age-grade.
In manhood training sessions, we recite out loud our lessons
A spear we can skillfully cast. We chant the glorious stories of our
past.
Poison darts we expertly throw. We can shoot an arrow through a
bow.
The trees, herbs and plants, we all know. But, a link seems missing
from my life that training cannot fulfill.
I need to put in practice, my well-learned skills."

The wise elder smiled and stared in his face.
"Brave minds like yours, will strengthen our race.
Between your destiny and your past lies that missing link.
When you discover your path in life, you shall not shrink …
But what's the matter little brother, please tell me what …
Why your eyes look big as two coconuts!"

"Down … there by the edge of the coast …
I thought I saw a man … that looked like a ghost!"

"Are you sure it was a man and not the sun's glare at noon?"

"I'm sure it was a man, but we'll know very soon."

"Did it have stringy yellow hair with cold, blue eyes?
Pale dry skin, with mouth full of eyes?
Did it carry a stick that shoots fire and round its neck wear a cross?!
They CAPTURE African people, and claim THEY are boss!
They STEAL our people away in the ships with big sails.
We know not where they take us,
But we've heard HORRENDOUS tales!"
"But, I don't understand my elder, what does this all mean?!
LISTEN…From the river, a distant SCREAM!!!"

"Look my brave young brother, you must hurry with your feet!
Back to our village, have the drummers start their beat.
Try and fly back home, quick as a bird.
Tell our people what, we've seen and heard!"

"But elder I hate to leave you with that limp in your knee.
Why don't you come too, and tell what we see?"

"Not yet little man, do as I say.
Danger is ahead, we did not heed The Way.
The ancestors warned in a foreign land we would toil,
If we let the paleface step on African soil!
I will peer through the shade of this baobab tree.
Then quickly limp back, to tell what I see!"

Running back home, quick as a gazelle.
To let the village know, that all is not well.
As the village hears the rhythmic talk of the drums
Beautiful ebony faces quickly come …

"Now little brother with eyes so serious.
What is your message, we are all very curious?
We trust it is important, what you have to say
For you had the drummers summon us in the midst of the day."

"I have just come from the river," exclaimed the brave young brother.
What I saw would make you shiver." "Oh no!" cried his mother.

"What did you see?" demanded a sister with a baby on her hip.

"I saw a paleface carrying a long fire stick!
And the elder that I met with the limp in his knee,
Said many years we ignored, the ancient prophecy."

"But where is he now?" questioned the sister with the baby on her
hip.

"By an old baobab tree, watching the paleface load his ship."

"Oh alas," moaned his mama. "We have strayed from The Way!
Destruction is now coming. To the gods we must pray!"

"We must FIGHT!" demanded a man with a spear in his hand.
"We must drive away the paleface from the shores of our land!"

"BEWARE!" whispered a grandmother. "The Ancestors foretold…
If we strayed from The Way we would be captured and sold!
The Ancient Ones warned in a foreign land we would toil
If we let the pale destroyers stop on African soil."

"But I've heard of an army," countered the man with the spear in his hand.
"It is led by a queen, who drives the paleface from our land!
This great Nzinga," he continued, "has the sticks that shoot fire.
Her army knows The Way, their resistance never tires.
She seeks new warriors, everywhere she goes.
I've pledged myself to fight, with hundreds I know."

"I want to help them!" shouted the young brother with braveness on his face.
"I want to join her army, to help save our race.
I think I've found the missing link, to fight I have the will.
I want to put in practice, my well-learned skills!"

"Oh NO!" screamed his mother, with fear in her eyes.
"If you fight you will surely, get hurt or die!"

"Seems wiser to try and fight to be free,
Than do nothing and be captured," argued a voice with a familiar ring.

Quickly looking around the lad was relieved to see,
The elder he had met with the limp in his knee.

"What did you see?" the people quizzed the elder with the limp in
his knee.
"Through the thick shield of an old baobab tree,
I saw hundreds of chained Africans, the paleface carried the key.
What I saw was the result of an ancient prophecy.
But the central question is, will OUR village remain free?"

"He is right," added a blind man, beginning to speak.
"Although I have no sight, I can plainly see."
Turning to the people, with awe in their eyes, he said
"What the warrior with the spear has pledged,
The young brother knows is wise."

The blind seer shakes some shells out of his hand.
Kneels to the ground, to feel how they land.
The towards the four winds and the sun bright and round
He speaks as his mind feels, the spirit's sound.

"Young brother you've almost finished, manhood training sessions.
The Ancestors make it known, you've studied well your lessons.
Many moons will soon pass, before you'll become a man.
But the spirits claim you'll FIGHT, to defend your land!

I know what will happen, although my eyes can't see.
I know what HAS happened in our glorious history
Long ago we all were wise, and closely followed The Way.
That when we GIVE, we also RECEIVE, that was the natural way

But as thousands of seasons danced slowly on,
Generations of us died, generations were reborn
And as those who followed not The Way, came to our shores to learn
We shared our knowledge with them, but they shared NOTHING in
return.

We taught them our ancient systems of mystery.
But they stole, destroyed, and plagiarized our history."

"But what of future seasons, blind man who sees with his mind?
What will be our destiny, what do your shells find?"

"Many villages will be destroyed," he said with a sad whisper.
They will march away Black mothers, fathers, brothers and sisters.
Because we failed to heed, the prophecy of old.
The warning that the ancient, soothsayers foretold.

**THAT WHEN WE GIVE, WE ALSO RECEIVE**
**AND NEVER BE FALSELY DECEIVED**
**FOR THE ANCESTORS HAD WARNED,**
**IN A FOREIGN LAND WE WOULD TOIL**
**IF WE LET THE PALEFACE STEP ON AFRICAN SOIL!"**

"But what about my son?!" wept the boy's disheartened mother.
"Will he be marched away, like so many others?"

"That I cannot say," replied the old blind man.
"But he WILL fight to save and defend our land.
ALL is not revealed to me, what his future will say.
But he will be a finder of new paths to our ancient Way."

Then the brave young brother embraced his mother,
And went to stand beside the man with the spear in his hand.

"And to all listening today," continued the wise blind man.
"I have one last thing to say. We all need to seek and re-find our
natural way.
But can that be done if we let the paleface stay?
It is time for all to go, and decide for yourselves THE WAY."

So all dispersed from the square to make their decision.
To determine what would now become their life's mission.
Knowing down by the coast awaits the paleface with his ship.
The sister gazed down upon the baby on her hip.
She then smiled proudly at the brother, with her arm around his
mother.
For she knew this day she had re-found THE WAY.
And in struggling to save their land, his mama would soon
understand

The blind man whose mind could see nodded and slowly hobbled
away
Alongside the elder with the limp in his knee
And the wise old grandmother departed,
Counseling The Way to many others

THEN FINALLY THE BRAVE YOUNG BROTHER
FELT THAT COMMON LINK
AND THE MAN WITH THE SPEAR IN HIS HAND GAVE HIM A WINK
AND BOTH KNEW THE WAY OF THEIR VILLAGE
WOULD BE TO DEFEND THEIR LAND!

# CINQUE AND THE AMISTAD

Amistad, the Amistad
The year was 1839
Rebellion on a slave ship
It was Liberation Time!

Amistad, the Amistad
A great thunderstorm's might
Loosened a nail in the slave-hold
Cinque unchained his people in the night

Bravely destroying their kidnappers with swords and a knife
Sparing only the navigator's life
Cinque smiled and cried, 'We are free of those beasts!'
To the navigator he ordered, 'We want Africa, steer east!'

But alas, traveling eastwards by day
The tricky navigator zigzagged westwards by night
And again into the clutches of slaveholders
Was the bold Africans plight

Now shackled and chained in an American jail
Were Cinque and the Amistad's Black crew
Oh how Cinque longed for that nail
And for the homeland in the East he once knew.

But finally after lengthy court trials and abolitionist debate
And since "legally" the slave trade was to have ended by 1808
Cinque and his mutineers were declared FREE
And most were returned to Africa, the home of their family tree.

Amistad, the Amistad
The year was 1839
Rebellion on a slave ship
**IT WAS LIBERATION TIME!**

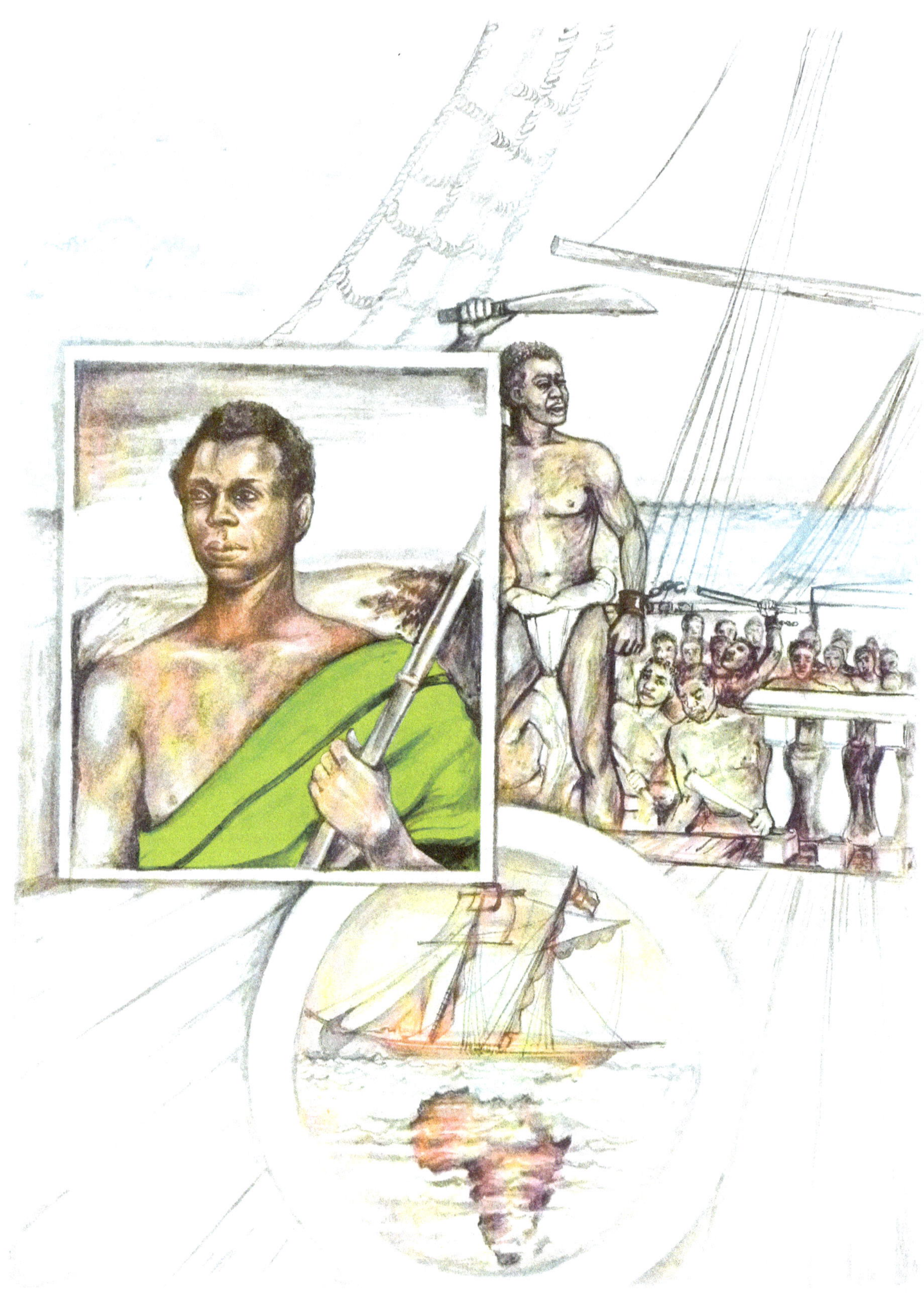

# THE SAGA OF TOUSSAINT L'OUVERTURE

If you look very closely on a map you will see
One of the little islands in what was called the West Indies
San Domingo was its name, many years ago
When Toussaint L'Ouverture became its hero

When Africans were kidnapped and sailed to western shores
They were first brought to these islands and whipped and tortured
Forced to cut the cane to the whip's stinging tune,
Many escaped to the hills to become the famous Maroons

As the Maroons from the hills, began to resist
The brothers in the fields also raised their fists
The struggle both began was more felt than seen
Til Toussaint L'Ouverture came on the scene

A leader he was, and a genius at that
As he made the Black Army sharp as a crack
The resistance Blacks waged put fear across the seas
For their purpose in life was to set their island free

L'Ouverture, Christophe, and Dessalines we should know
Led this great revolution in San Domingo
Their struggle was to remove oppression from their land
And to build a Black Republic where dignity might stand

So Toussaint L'Ouverture, to set his island free
Outwitted the Spanish, British and French armies
And because the Blacks were winning, France was forced to sell
Almost half the land America boasts of so well

Cause Toussaint really put those French in a pinch
From the British, he got what he wished
The army of Spain, Toussaint put in pain
Now control was in the Black folk's domain.

CUBA
SAN DOMINGO
JAMAICA

L'Ouverture, Christophe and Dessalines we should know
Led this great revolution in San Domingo
Their struggle was to remove, oppression from their land
And to build a Black Republic where dignity might stand

But in every great genius, there is a tragic flaw
L'Ouverture's flaw was that he held the French diplomacy as law
So because he put his trust in his enemy's word
He viciously was tricked, and to France he was lured

As he died in the cold, damp French dungeon cell
Dessalines continued The Struggle, and sent the slavers to hell

Now no more toiling for another person's gain
No more whips to cut the cane
And because they strived for a complete victory
They changed the island's name to become HAITI

L'Ouverture, Christophe and Dessalines we should know
Led this great revolution in San Domingo
Their struggle was to remove, oppression from their land
And to build a Black Republic where dignity might stand

But this first Black Republic in the Western Hemisphere
Would be ruthlessly destabilized over the years
So we must always keep in mind, the struggle of the three
And return the island Haiti to what they fought for it to be!

The time is always
right to do right

Dr. Martin Luther King Jr.

# THE LEGEND OF DENMARK VESEY

This is the legend of Denmark Vesey
His tale will last to the end of time
Though the life of the enslaved was never easy
He became a brilliant Black mastermind!

South Carolina is where this story takes place
The time was during slavery
'Tho we planted the fields with a smile on our face
Black bodies were itching to be free

In Vesey's day in South Caroline
The slaveholder's life was lazy and fine
Horseraces, cockfights, slave auctions and balls
They never dreamed of a revolt to make them fall

Meanwhile, one day Vesey won a lottery game
And with the winnings all in his name
Went straight to his owner cuz he had the right fee
Gave him the money and bought himself free

Vesey learned the trade of carpentry
And became very learned and skilled
But he felt and saw that Blacks although free
Were still harassed, beaten and killed

**AS VESEY LOOKED AROUND AND FELT THE BLACK
ENSLAVED PLIGHT
HE KNEW THAT FREEDOM BOUGHT WAS NOT QUITE RIGHT**

So, one evening at a secret meeting he declared
"It is high time we had OUR share!
If it be freedom and land we really desire
We MUST be willing to fight fire with fire!"

Now inspired by the recent Haitian revolution
Vesey felt he had found the only solution
To rise up the enslaved and slay the racist Whites
And build a Black nation to set things right

Hence gathering six others in absolute trust
Making Peter Poyas his right hand man
Secrecy was to be an absolute must
If they were to succeed in Freeing the Land

Also Ned and Rolla, the Governor's slaves
Were in this bold plan for Blacks
Monday Gell and Mingo Hearth
And the Angolan sorcerer, Gullah Jack

Carpenters, blacksmiths, shipbuilders by day
Plotters of bold strategies by night
Vesey and his team planned a slave uprising
That would place the slaveholders in utter fright

Vesey the mastermind often proclaimed
"We need to disguise our revolutionary aims
We must mask our feelings, hide our goals
We must play the docile, contented role"

Then Peter Poyas told all to heed
This warning so their plan would be sure to succeed
'Beware of slaves eating scraps from massa's table
Slaves wearing massa's old clothes
Only recruit those whose minds are able
Those who've felt slavery's bitter woes'

Secret lists were kept of all new recruits
For the plan was rapidly bearing ripe fruit
Instructions were made for all lists to be burned
If knowledge of the rebellion too early is learned

And as Vesey was rappin' to add a name to a list
An example of the talk might have gone like this …

'But from where,' asked Ben, 'would we get the men?'
'Oh we'd get them easy,' replied Vesey
'From the country and the town
ALL the Blacks will come down'

'But how,' questioned Ben, 'will we know when to begin?'
And Vesey whispered… 'The 16th of June
Will be slavery's doom
At the stroke of midnight, the Blacks will strike!'

'But what of the slaveholder's children
Should they also be hit?'
'Do you think it wise,' replied Vesey
'To destroy the louse and leave the nit?!'

'But what,' demanded Ben, 'Will we do for arms?
The slaveholders have the most effective methods of harm'

'Arsenals, armories and guardhouses,' Vesey confided
'Will be our first point of attack
Then we will set South Carolina on fire
And there will be, NO TURNING BACK'

'Now, are you convinced?' asked Vesey
'How do you stand?'
Ben answered with a clenched fist, stating
'Firm as this, my man!'

So, over 9000 stood ready, waitin' for the night
When Blacks would take over the land to make things right

But alas in their wall of secrecy there became a crack
Which would send terrified slave owners onto their track
The warning of Poyas should have been heeded
Then the rebellion of 1822 might have succeeded

Unfortunately one brother felt the fighting would go faster
If he told ALL Blacks he could
Then a house slave in turn, informed his slave master
Just as Poyas always warned they would.

So, bits of the plot leaked out
Pieces of the plan were revealed
Vesey tried to pretend no conspiracy was in the wind
But by now the fate of the revolt was sealed

Luckily as the lists were burned
Many names were never learned
But the lazy livin' of southern Whites
Was now a storm of thundering fright

The record claims they arrested one hundred thirty-one
Tried them and hung thirty-five
Whites questioned, but answers were few to none
So many of the 9000 revolters stayed alive.

Peter Poyas had told all, 'Do not open your lips!
Even if you are tortured and whipped
For if you do, many more will be captured too
Die silent, as you shall see me do!'

All but one remained strong to the end
And when hung did not shed a tear
Although this revolt Blacks did not win
All knew the next one would be near

And to this very day all the facts are not known
About this plan Vesey had been organizing
But we do all know, that nine years later…
**Nat Turner led a MEAN – UPRISING!**

# HARRIET WAS STRONG, SHE NEVER WENT WRONG

Listen to the legend of Harriet Tubman
For you will see what strength is all about
That she was a warrior in every sense of the word
There is definitely no doubt

Born in Maryland on the Eastern Shore
A strong field enslaved person was she
She worked so hard 'til her bones were sore
But she always yearned to be free

When Harriet was young she was hit on the head
With a two-pound iron weight
She fell to the floor, they thought she was dead
But she lived to become quite great

Now scarred with a large dent in her skull
It took months to get well again
Even though she regained her strength once more
She had sleeping spells now and then

One night Harriet said she would take this no more
And decided it was time to escape
She fled through fields and farms, past plantations and barns
'Til she reached North where she could stay

But while "free" in the North, she had few friends
For they were all still in the South
So she worked very hard and with the money she saved
She went back South to free hundreds of the enslaved

Though Harriet was SMALL
Her mission was TALL
She had to be brave, to set free the enslaved
**HARRIET WAS STRONG, SHE NEVER WENT WRONG**

WANTED
DEAD OR ALIVE
HARRIET TUBMAN
REWARD
$40,000
SLAVE
KIDNAPPER.

Though Harriett was wanted, DEAD or ALIVE
She kept on pushing
She took no jive
**HARRIET WAS STRONG, SHE NEVER WENT WRONG**

She trudged back South, NINETEEN TIMES
To lead three hundred North
They waded through streams; they scaled high mountains
But they NEVER STOPPED going forth

They followed the moss on the side of the trees
For they knew it led North; it was Nature's key
They followed the North Star, for it was a Guide
By Moon they would travel; by Sun they would hide

For all to stay alive Harriet carried a forty-five
And if any tried to leave
She quickly removed it from her sleeve
**HARRIET WAS STRONG, SHE NEVER WENT WRONG**

When the enslaved heard they were to be sold
They sought the Underground Railroad
Closely they listened for Harriet's song
For when it came, they would be gone

What was this Underground Railroad?
Was it a REAL train with tracks?
Oh no, but the Underground Railroad
Was a secret escape system for Blacks

The ART of escape was a dangerous one
As they traveled in disguise
By boat, by wagon, by foot, by carriage
She vowed, 'No One Will Take Us Back Alive!'

To Pennsylvania and New York she brought the enslaved
'Til these states were safe no more
Then all the way to Canada she trudged
Where her people would be enslaved no more

She could not read, nor could she write
But THOUSANDS of times, She OUTWITTED the Whites
Like Nzinga before, and Assata after
**HARRIET WAS STRONG, SHE NEVER WENT WRONG**

**HARRIET WAS STRONG, SHE NEVER WENT WRONG!**

# SOJOURNER'S TRUTH

Sojourn means to journey a long way
Truth means to speak no lies
Put them together and what do they say?
Sojourner Truth, now wasn't that wise!

Sister Sojourner born in this country enslaved
But that did not shut her mouth
The truth about slavery she did not save
Carried her message from the North to the South

Sojourn means to journey a long way
Truth means to speak no lies
Put them together and what do they say?
Sojourner Truth, now wasn't that wise?

She spoke of the evils of slavery
And of all human beings' rights
Tellin' the truth showed her bravery
And that she was not afraid to fight

Sojourn means to journey a long way
Truth means to speak no lies
Put them together and what do they say?
**Sojourner Truth, NOW WASN'T THAT WISE!**

# THE MIGHTY MARCUS GARVEY

The mighty Marcus Garvey if you have ever seen
Was the proud Black man with the Red, Black and Green
The mighty Marcus Garvey had a lot of pride
Millions of Black folk were on his side

He sailed from Jamaica to New York City
He organized a group in the 1920's
The Universal Negro Improvement Association
To millions was a great inspiration

He had the Black Cross Nurses
That worked so fine
The Black Legionnaires
And the Black Star Line

The Black Star Line was the name of the ships
They would trade with Black Nations and make many trips
The Black Legionnaires was the army-to-be
They trained to fight to set Black people free

The mighty Marcus Garvey had big parades
The foundation of our nation was being laid
The mighty Marcus Garvey had a lot of pride
Millions of Black folk were on his side

He said African people were a mighty race
But we need once more a mighty land base
Let AFRICA be our guiding star
And then we'll know freedom won't be far

But some brainwashed Blacks turned up their nose
The racist court system said 'Garvey has to Go!'
Back to Jamaica he was finally sent
But as he went he left, us this hint

'Look for me in the whirlwind,' he said
'Look for me in the storm
Look for me all around you
For my spirit will bring freedom to form'

The mighty Marcus Garvey if you have ever seen
Was the proud Black man with the Red, Black and Green
Millions of Black folk were on his side
**'Cause the mighty Marcus Garvey HAD A LOT OF PRIDE!**

# CELEBRATING PAUL ROBESON

We need to celebrate the story of Paul Robeson
Who was one of the greatest Black towers of our race
He maintained his strength and pride 'til his life was done
His struggle we have not begun to taste

Paul Robeson did well his lessons in school
Paul Robeson sang strong in harmonic tunes
Paul Robeson acted all over the world in plays
But Paul Robeson never strayed from his positive Black ways

We need to celebrate the story of Paul Robeson
We need to speak loudly his name
In the face of racism, in the face of danger
He spoke out, he didn't care about fame

Paul Robeson's struggle was in the 1930's
When Jim Crow nearly brought Blacks to our knees
But Paul Robeson loudly protested segregation
And for that his career was seized

We need to celebrate the name of Paul Robeson
For his fame was great indeed
Not only in his lessons, singing and acting
But also in planting us a seed

A seed of Black pride and power
A seed of strong determination
A seed that is growing into a tower
A tower of Black Liberation

We need to celebrate the story of Paul Robeson
Who was one of the greatest giants of our race
He maintained his strength and pride 'til his life was done
His struggle we have not begun to taste.

# HER NAME WAS FANNIE LOU HAMER

Her name was Fannie Lou Hamer, born in 1917
Grandma had been enslaved, and the times were still mean

The state was Mississippi, Ruleville was the place
Where Blacks sharecropped the land, for another people's race

Now the "owner" of this land was a farmer who was slick

Cause he devised a little scheme when Fannie Lou was six

Promising her whatever she wanted from his store
She had to pick 30 pounds of cotton or more

Though he gave her what he promised, that sly slick day
He now knew that she could work, gone were childhood days of play

So as a little girl she labored picking cotton for the Whites
From "can't see in the morning," 'til "can't see at night"
When Fannie went to school she learned readin' and writin'
Songs she always sang and poems she loved recitin'

But Fannie always felt the grim hardness of Black life
And she wished that she could change it, and make conditions bright

Later falling in love she married Perry "Pap" Hamer
But conditions in the South could make her life no tamer

Terror reigned all over and from places Blacks were barred
All because of the racist, Mississippi laws

So when the protestors came in the summer of '62
They showed Black folk of Ruleville, that Blacks had rights too

Listening to these words gave Fannie a little light of hope
As she learned that Blacks too, had a right to vote

But when they went to the court to try to register to vote
They found the test given to Blacks had bearings of a hoax

Being ridiculous, racist, and quite unfair
This registration test was more than Fannie Lou could bear

All Blacks failed the test that day with hearts beginning to burn
But they refused to give up, and vowed they would return

The following year Fannie passed that voting test
And she worked in The Movement, with quite a lot of zest

Now an activist for SNCC she began to speak and organize
Taught constitutional rights and exposed the country's lies

But for working to help others pass the voting test
She was detained, questioned, then placed under arrest

Beaten 'til her body was battered and told that she would die
The kicks left her kidney injured and a blood clot in her eye

Because of being harassed, threatened, and from her job fired
Fannie Lou often said she was just 'sick and tired of being sick and tired'

But never did she give up that little light of hope
But kept right on registering Black folk to vote

Speaking all over the country she was determined to the core
Protested cruel conditions of Blacks as well as the Viet Nam War

Her powerful voice led many a great freedom song
Giving inspiration to millions while detailing America's wrongs

Now this sister also had a tremendous bit of wit
'If you give a man food he will eat it,' she would say
But if you're serious about setting the self-sufficiency tone
'Give a man LAND so he can grow his own!'

Her proverb rallied round the South like a beckoning horn
Thus the Freedom Farm Cooperative was born

Though shot at, threatened, and beaten by the Klan
Over 5000 came to Mississippi to work on the land

Although the Klan interfered with the building of the Farm
They were not the only group to cause the Black folk harm

The Democrats of 'Sippi had a party of all Whites
They refused to let Blacks join and denied them equal rights

So because the 'Sippi Democrats would not be integrated
Fannie had the Mississippi Freedom Democratic Party created

While at the Democratic Convention Fannie tried to get seated
But the racist Mississippians had her Freedom Party defeated

But because she was determined to stand up for Black rights
The Convention gave the order that the 'Crats could not stay White

So because the Party refused to let Blacks participate
Fannie's Freedom Party was seated at the Convention in '68

Because of her strength, determination, and total lack of fear
Fannie Lou won many honors and awards over the years

In March of '77, she passed from this life
The work she had done served to lessen Black folk's strife

Though Blacks had had the worst of times in struggling for the vote
Fannie Lou Hamer never gave up that little light of hope!

# THE BALLAD OF ROSA PARKS

Sister Rosa Parks, strong and bold
She was standin' by the bus stop courageous and cold
Along came the bus with its Jim Crow laws
Seemed like a prison with invisible bars

Well Rosa Parks got on that bus and started toward the back
Where the Alabama law said was the place for Blacks
Looking in the back she didn't see any seats
So she sat down near the front; she had destiny to meet

Sister Rosa Parks, strong and bold
Sat calm and determined like an ancient queen of gold
When the bus driver came and demanded her seat
She refused to obey and stand to her feet

'Look here gal, don't you know the laws of this land?!
Blacks got to get up for every White man!"
'I refuse to give up my seat
I paid my fare like all on this bus
I'll remain strong if you beat me
I'll remain strong because I must'

'Police, police, arrest this woman now
Throw her in the jail, she's a threat to this town!'

Rosa looked around and thought it just wasn't fair
But the people acted like they just didn't care

But there were folk in the community
Who were practicing Black unity
And at a big meeting that night
They discussed the bus plight

'If Blacks stop riding the buses,' said a brother
'The bus company will lost a lot of money,' said another
'A bus boycott sounds like a good way,' said a sister
'They sure don't need to get rich off OUR pay,' said a mister

So they got Rosa Parks out of the Alabama jail
And all had faith that their plan would not fail
Then no bus in Montgomery did Black people ride
Because it took away their African dignity and pride

Rosa organized wagons, bicycles, car pools and mules
So Blacks, young and old, could get to work and to school
And with the leader they elected Rev. Martin Luther King
Black people walked all that winter, summer, fall and spring

So finally the state was forced
To change the laws it had made
Because while Blacks stayed off the buses
The company didn't get paid

But some groups did not like this
One was called the Ku Klux Klan
And they threatened Rosa Parks
With their evil, devilish plans

But sister Rosa Parks was strong and bold
She had **STOOD** by that bus stop courageous and cold
When she thought of the Klan and how they hate
She knew if she had to do it again
**SHE WOULD NOT HESITATE!**

________________________________

You must never
be fearful about
what you are doing
when it is right."

Rosa Parks

# JOHN COLTRANE PLAYED ALL THAT JAZZ

John Coltrane played all that jazz
Black genius of the saxophone
Great Black Music with lots of class
Messages with musical tone

His horn always blew "My Favorite Things"
He gave us "A Love Supreme"
"Ascensions" sounds from a Black King
"Naima" was his praise for a Queen

He learned from Charlie Parker the Bird
Because of Bird, Trane's music is heard

Trane inspired Pharaoh's "Creator Has a Master Plan"
To spread peace and happiness throughout the land

The autumn equinox was when Coltrane was born
They say he came out blowing on a golden horn
"Ooh la la" and "Africa's Brass"
Great Black Music which they called jazz

He had "A Song of the Underground Railroad"
And one called "Chasing the Trane"
"Dear Lord" and "Meditations" eased our load
"Alabama" was for four who were slain

Always remember John Coltrane
They say he was the Malcolm X of jazz
Brother Malcolm's message reached us
Just as Coltrane's has

Malcolm X preached Black facts
We heard what he had to say
John Coltrane preached on a sax
We heard in his own creative way

Positive themes emitted from his sax
Balance was where Trane's mind was at
"Dahomey Dance," "Reverend King" and "Afro-Blue"
Spiritual, Cultural and Political Tunes

John Coltrane played all that jazz
Black genius of the saxophone
Great Black Music with lots of class
Messages with musical tone

Do YOU remember John Coltrane?
Cause his music sure was strong
ALWAYS remember John Coltrane
Then our Nation stays strong!

# THE SAGA OF MALCOLM X

**MALCOLM X WAS A STRONG BLACK MAN
MALCOLM X SAID THE STRUGGLE'S FOR LAND
SELF-DETERMINATION FOR BLACK PEOPLE NOW
BY ANY MEANS NECESSARY WAS HIS VOW**

He was born Malcolm Little on the 19th day
1925, the month was May
He was born up South in Omaha, Nebraska
Even before his birth there was much disaster

Around his father's home the Klan did ride
Mama and children were alone inside
Because the Rev. Little was away that night
The Klan got away without a fight

The family moved to Lansing, Michigan
Malcolm's father bought a house but there was violence again
Because Rev. Little organized for the U.N.I.A.
The Klan burned their home one dreadful day

When Malcolm was six he took a deep long breath
It was whispered his father had just been beat to death
Attacked by White racists and thrown across the tracks
Because he stood up for what Garvey taught about Blacks

The state broke up his home, drove his mama out of her mind
She was sent to the hospital; her children were in a bind
Now Malcolm being young and without parental guide
He began to steal, he cheated and lied

But at the state detention home where Malcolm was sent
He made good grades and was class president
Then when asked in school what he wished to be
'A lawyer,' Malcolm said quite proudly
His teacher looked at him and said, 'You're out of your mind
A simpler type of work you had better find!'
Malcolm was discouraged from that point on
Lost interest in school and in eighth grade was gone

He traveled to Boston to live with his sister Ella
Became a shoeshine boy and a hip slick fella
Malcolm learned how to hustle, how to make a quick buck
Caught the train to Harlem and thought he'd found luck

At Small's Paradise he got a waiter's job
He met many gangsters and learned more ways to rob
'Big Red' was the nickname he was called
Cause he had reddish-brown hair and was six feet tall

Malcolm broke into houses late at night
Stole clothes and jewelry, whatever he could sight
Was caught by police and sent to jail
He was 20 years old but given no bail

At first in prison Malcolm acted really mean
They called him 'Satan' cause he made an evil scene
But a few years later he took a long curious look
In the prison library and checked out a book

Malcolm hadn't read a book since the eighth grade
But he copied down the words, page after page
After the dim prison lights were out in his cell
Malcolm read until his eyes were no longer well

He studied about Africa and its ancient glories
He studied about Blacks, and read many stories
He went though the dictionary and learned much knowledge
Later on many would think he had been to college

While studying in prison Malcolm wrote many letters
His brother often visited him to make him feel better
This brother spoke with pride about a religion he had embraced
He said the Nation of Islam was for the Black race

The Honorable Elijah Muhammad was the leader of the group
It uplifted Black folk and taught them the truth
Now Malcolm listened closely to what his brother said
Many years had passed since he was called "Big Red"

He began to write Muhammad and the Messenger wrote back
Elijah taught him facts about Whites and Blacks
He wrote him of devilish deeds by the racist White man
About the tricks and the lies, he spread throughout the land

Malcolm slowly thought back and remembered his past
Those who messed up his life hard and fast
The Klan who laid his pa across the tracks
The teacher who said a lawyer was not for Blacks

The judge who sentenced him away to do time
The state which drove his mama, out of her mind
That he must struggle against evil was now plain to see
Malcolm now knew what he wanted his life to be

So when Malcolm left jail in 1952
He changed his ways, he had work to do
He smoked no cigarettes, sold no dope
Because being a Muslim gave him hope

Now remember at his birth his last name was Little?
Where the name came from no longer was a riddle
'Twas the slave owner's name from long ago
So Malcolm used an 'X' for the name he'd never know

Malcolm became a Muslim minister
The Nation of Islam was at its peak
Malcolm founded new temples
And the paper "Muhammad Speaks"

He often talked on street corners, and in the bars
And to the hustlers with the big, fine flashy cars
And he rapped to Black youth with respect in their eyes
As he showed how integration seemed like slavery in disguise

Malcolm spoke of self-defense and independent land
About human rights that Blacks must demand
He became a great leader, very busy was his life
He made fiery speeches, now had children and a wife

But it was later found out that the vicious F.B.I.
Joined Black groups to destroy and spy
Soon the once strong movement became infiltrated
Elijah Muhammad and Malcolm X were soon separated

So Malcolm traveled to Mecca, and Ghana too
Then came back to Harlem to found the O.A.A.U.
He said fighting for just civil rights will not let us rise
To win our struggle **INTERNATIONALIZE!**

Just to hear this great Black man, made the people fascinated
But also there were those who, wanted him assassinated …
Very busy Malcolm stayed as the months passed along
Although his life was now in danger, he kept on pushing on

But February twenty-first, nineteen sixty-five
Was the last day Malcolm was to stay alive
About to make a speech Malcolm faced his doom
Up on the stage of Harlem's Audubon Ballroom

Now in this audience were some men who did what Whites willed
They aimed their shotguns, and Malcolm was **KILLED**
People mourned Malcolm's death all over this land
They loved him cause they knew he was a **STRONG BLACK MAN**

Since then his body has rested, six feet underground
But across the Black Nation, his spirit can be found
Though the vision Malcolm gave us was so very strong
His message can be found, in this little song …

**MALCOLM X WAS A STRONG BLACK MAN**
**MALCOLM X SAID THE STRUGGLE'S FOR LAND**
**SELF-DETERMINATION FOR BLACK PEOPLE NOW**
**BY ANY MEANS NECESSARY WAS HIS VOW!**

---

There is no excuse for the
young people not knowing who
their heroes and heroines are or were.

Nina Simone, singer

# AFRICAN PROVERBS

1. Wisdom outweighs strength

2. If you are greedy in conversation you lose the wisdom of your friend

3. You send a wise person on an important mission, not a long-legged person

4. The wise person who does not learn ceases to be wise

5. When a fowl is eating your neighbor's corn, drive it away or someday it will eat yours

6. It is easier to put out a fire in the house of a neighbor than to deal with the smoke in one's own.

7. One should not ignore an elephant and throw stones at a small bird

8. Children are the wealth of a nation

9. The moon moves slowly but it crosses the town

10. When a cock is drunk he forgets about the hawk

11. Home affairs are not talked about on the public square

12. When the mouse laughs at the cat, there is a hole nearby

13. If you are building a house and a nail breaks, do you stop building, or do you change the nail?

14. No matter how long the night, the day is sure to come

15. He who digs too deep for a fish may come out with a snake

16. Confiding a secret to an unworthy person is like carrying grain in a bag with a hole

17. Cross the river in a crowd and the crocodile won't eat you

18. No one tests the depth of a river with both feet

19. He who is bitten by a snake fears a lizard

20. Only when you have crossed the river can you say the crocodile has a lump on his snout

21. Two birds disputed over a kernel when a third swooped down and carried it off

22. Wood may remain ten years in water but it will never become a crocodile

23. It is better to know your own faults than those of your neighbor

24. A child may have as many clothes as his father, but he does not have as many rags

25. The hand of a child cannot reach the shelf, nor can the hand of an adult get through the neck of a gourd

26. One who fetches water at the same place on the riverbank too often ends up in the crocodile

# GLOSSARY

This glossary attempts to give meanings to the words in this book in as simple a way as possible. For more detailed definitions, please consult other sources.

**Africa:** the second largest continent in the world; it has been called the birthplace of civilization

**Age-grade:** an African system of classifying young people

**Amistad:** a Spanish word meaning "friendship." Ironically, it was the name of a slave ship

**Ancestors:** departed relatives whose spirits are around to assist the living

**Ancient:** long, long ago

**Arms:**  another word for weapons

**Arsenal:** a place for making and storing military weapons

**Assassination:** the killing of an important person

**Baobab:** a broad-trunked tropical tree found in Africa.

**Boycott:** when one stops doing something in protest of something else

**Brainwashed**: indoctrination or persuasion to have one believe what you wish them to believe

**Compound:** a type of dwelling place

**Conspiracy:** an agreement by persons to do an unlawful act

**Destabilize:** disrupting a country to make it lose its balance

**Diplomacy:** the art of speaking and getting one's point across effectively

**Docile:** easily managed or handled, readily trained

**Elder:** an older person

**Equinox:** the time when the sun crosses the equator and day and night are in equal length

**FBI:** an abbreviation for the Federal Bureau of Investigation. A U.S. agency that collects information of people

**Flaw:** a weak point in one's character

**Forty-five:** a type of gun

**Ghana:** a country in West Africa

**Harlem:** a section of New York City where many Black people have lived

**Harvest:** the time of gathering in the crops previously planted

**Infiltrate:** to join an organization under false pretenses. The group does not know who you really are

**Internationalize:** to bring before other nations and countries in the world

**Jamaica:** an island in the Caribbean

**Jim Crow laws:** discriminatory laws restricting things Black people could do in the U.S.

**Ku Klux Klan:** a terrorist white organization believing that the white people are better than other people

**Labored:** worked

**Liberation:** another word for freedom.

**Maroons:** formerly enslaved people who escaped and set up communities in the hills

**Mecca:** a holy city in Saudi Arabia where Muslims journey to

**Montgomery:** the capitol of the state of Alabama

**Mourn:** to feel or express grief or sorrow

**Muslim:** a person who follows the Islamic religion

**Navigator:** one who steers a ship

**Nzinga:** an African queen who fought for many years to keep the Portuguese from capturing her people to become enslaved

**O.A.A.U.:** abbreviation for the Organization for Afro-American Unity; the organization Malcolm X started after he left the Nation of Islam

**Plagiarize:** taking credit for something that someone else has done first

**Prophecy:** a prediction about something to occur in the future

**Proverb:** a wise saying

**Racist:** one who believes his or her race is superior to or better than others

**Recruit:** newly enlisted, one who has joined something

**Redemption:** to take back

**Revolution:** a change in government or the social order

**Satan:** another name for the devil

**Seer:** one who can see and tell the future

**Segregation**: to set apart from the rest in a discriminatory fashion

**Self-Defense:** protecting oneself against attacks

**Self-Determination:** the ability of a people to decide for themselves what they want to do with their lives

**Self-sufficiency:** not depending on anyone for the things one needs to survive

**Sharecrop:** when one works another's land in return for a share of the crop

**SNCC:** abbreviation for the Student Non-Violent Coordinating Committee; it was a civil rights organization that later changed its name to the Student National Coordinating Committee

**Soothsayer:** one who foretells events

**U.N.I.A.:** abbreviation for the Universal Negro Improvement Association, the organization founded by Marcus Garvey

**Whirlwind:** a small, rotating windstorm

# REVIEW QUESTIONS AND WORK PROJECTS

### AGES 5 through 7

1. Ask the oldest person in your family if they have ever heard of Marcus Garvey. If not, read them the storypoem and discuss with them this great Black man.

2. Read the definition of "boycott" in the glossary.  Why did Black people in Montgomery, Alabama boycott the buses in 1955?

3. Explain in your own words what the underground railroad was.

### AGES 8 through 10

1. Using the "Ballad of Rosa Parks" as a guide, gather some friends together and act out different scenes from the storypoem.

2. Look up the definition of the following forms of creative writing: epic, legend, ballad, and saga, and relate them to the storypoems in this book.

3. What organizations do the following abbreviations stand for? OAAU, SNCC, UNIA

### AGES 11 and over

1. Research major slave rebellions in the U.S., the Underground Railroad, and Black speakers against enslavement. With the information you have compiled, write a comprehensive essay entitled "Black Resistance to Enslavement."

2. Using the storypoem "Her Name Was Fannie Lou Hamer," look at current news and analyze any similarities or differences between the denial of voting rights during her era, and the onslaught against voting rights today.

3. There are two distinct instances in the storypoems where Black people were betrayed. Name the two storypoems, cite the instances, and discuss what could have happened had betrayal not occurred.

4. Paul Robeson was a multi-talented individual. Read the storypoem, "Paul Robeson – A Celebration," research his life, and write an essay detailing not only his accomplishments, but also his stances against oppression.

It is not light we need, but fire. Not the gently
shower but thunder. We need the storm,
the whirlwind, and the earthquake.


Frederick Douglass, abolitionist, orator

# ABOUT THE AUTHOR

Nkechi Taifa is an attorney, activist, educator, author and mother. She is the author of several books for young people: *Shining Legacy: Storypoems for the Young, So Black Heroes and Heroines Forever Will be Sung*; *The Adventures of Kojo and Ama*; *Three Tales of Wisdom*; *New Afrikan Children of the Sun* (co-authored with Imamu Kuumba), and *Aisha and the Magic Ankh*. These classics were originally written while teaching at an Independent Black School during the late 1970's and some have now been re-published for a new generation. Taifa is also the author of the best-seller memoir – *Black Power, Black Lawyer: My Audacious Quest for Justice*, and a forthcoming book on reparations.

## ABOUT THE ILLUSTRATOR

Mary E. Mudiku (Maesgara) is an artist, poet, art therapist, workshop facilitator and prison program developer in recidivism reduction. She specializes in culture-based "Liberation Visualization" Creative Expression.

Original Black and White Illustrations Colorized by FreeBenJamin.com

# THE TAIFA TRILOGY OF TALES FOR A NEW GENERATION

## SHINING LEGACY:

### Storypoems For The Young, So Black Heroes And Heroines Forever Will Be Sung

*(Ages: 8 yrs old and up)*

Shining Legacy celebrates the past through epic, ballad, legend and saga, all accentuated with rhyme. Role models range from Harriet Tubman, Rosa Parks, Fannie Lou Hamer, and Sojourner Truth – to Malcolm X, Denmark Vesey, Toussaint L'Ouverture, Paul Robeson, and Marcus Garvey.

## THE ADVENTURES OF KOJO AND AMA

*(Ages: 5 yrs old – 12 yrs old)*

Journey with Kojo and Ama through seven adventures combining excitement, fun and suspense with lessons in pride and heritage. The children's heroic black cat Sheba brings them good luck as they find themselves in settings ranging from an inner city park to the deep South, and from the island of Jamaica to ancient Egypt.

## THREE TALES OF WISDOM

*(Ages: 8 yrs old and up)*

Anansi's magic helps Ayanna get to the Harvest Festival, despite the fact that her two sisters fail to follow the Seven Principles of the value system …

A young brother growing up in New York City learns the story of the mighty Marcus Garvey …

Jabari finds wisdom through his encounters with spiders, lions, warriors, elephants, cockroaches, camels and birds …

Master Storyteller *Nkechi Taifa* resurrects and republishes her popular books for young people from over three decades ago as she brings her timeless wisdom for new generations to enjoy.

# NOTES

# NOTES

**"Nea Onnim No Sua A, Ohu"**
Adinkra symbol meaning "he who does not know, can know"
is the symbol of knowledge, life-long education,
and continued quest for knowledge

www.ingramcontent.com/pod-product-compliance
Lightning Source LLC
Chambersburg PA
CBHW080910190726
48294CB00008B/2039